AT THE
CONSTRUCTION SITE

by Samantha Brooke
Illustrated by Jim Durk

Published by Scholastic Inc., 557 Broadway, New York, NY 10012. SCHOLASTIC and associated logos are trademarks and/or registered trademarks of Scholastic Inc.

ISBN 978-0-545-55028-4

12 11 10 9 8 7 6 5 4 3 2   13 14 15 16 17/0
Printed in the U.S.A.   40
First printing, September 2013

SCHOLASTIC INC.

These construction  are ready to build a new  .

They need lots of  to get the job done. Each worker also needs a , , , and a .

The worker puts on a .

This is going to get messy.

This is attached to a .

The knocks down the old

 .

Once the is knocked down,

the  bring in the

The will push the ,

 , , and  into a

big pile.

Then the 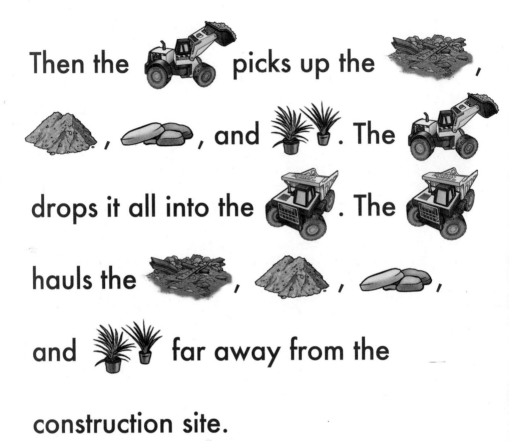 picks up the , , , and . The drops it all into the . The hauls the , , , and far away from the construction site.

Now it's time to roll in the  .

The digs a deep hole in the .

The and work together

again to remove the and

 .

Now the  can lay the

foundation for the  .

Cement is mixed in the of the

 . The turns and turns.

Then the pours out the wet

cement.

Here comes a  . It is carrying heavy _____ .

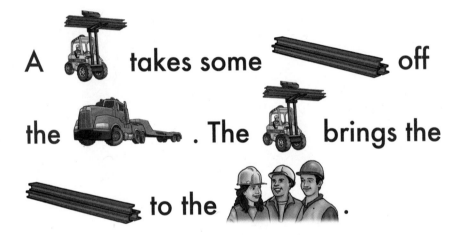

A _____ takes some _____ off the _____ . The _____ brings the _____ to the _____ .

The 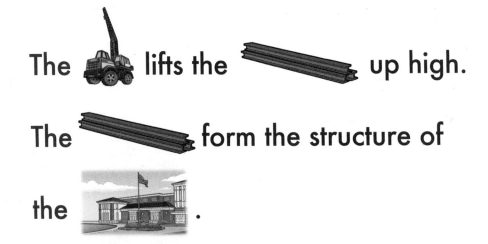 lifts the up high.

The form the structure of

the .

When all the  are in place,

the lifts up windows and dry wall.

Meanwhile, the flattens the around the  .

Then the pours out cement to make the sidewalk.

The  put new in the .

The  still have a lot of work

to do. Each worker gets out a ,

 ,  , and a .

The  also put in power lines

using a special truck called a cherry

picker.

The  is finished! The

put away every and ,

and all the  and .

The children from the  thank

the . Then the

and  drive away. It's a job

well done.

Did you spot all the picture clues in this book?

Each picture clue is on a flash card. Ask a grown-up to cut out the flash cards. Then try reading the words on the backs of the cards. The pictures will be your clues.

Reading is fun with Tonka!

school	workers
hammer	trucks
screws	nails

hard hat	drill
crane	wrecking ball
bulldozer	building

dirt	metal
plants	rocks
dump truck	loader

drum	excavator
flatbed truck	cement mixer
forklift	metal beams